P9-DOA-720

HOW BIG IS BIG?

For Jon and Jamie

PUFFIN BOOKS
Published by the Penguin Group
Penguin Books USA Inc., 375 Hudson Street, New York, New York 10014, U.S.A.
Penguin Books Ltd, 27 Wrights Lane, London W8 5TZ, England
Penguin Books Australia Ltd, Ringwood, Victoria, Australia
Penguin Books Canada Ltd, 10 Alcorn Avenue, Toronto, Ontario, Canada M4V 3B2
Penguin Books (N.Z.) Ltd, 182-190 Wairau Road, Auckland 10, New Zealand

Penguin Books Ltd, Registered Offices: Harmondsworth, Middlesex, England

First published in the United States of America by Viking Penguin Inc., 1989
Published simultaneously in a Puffin edition
Published in a Puffin Easy-to-Read edition, 1995

1 3 5 7 9 10 8 6 4 2

The Library of Congress has cataloged the Puffin books edition under
catalog card number 88-62151.

Puffin Easy-to-Read ISBN 0-14-037653-4

Puffin® and Easy-to-Read® are registered trademarks of Penguin Books USA Inc.
Printed in the United States of America

Reading Level 1.6

HOW BIG IS BIG?

Harriet Ziefert
Pictures by Andrea Baruffi

PUFFIN BOOKS

What's big?
Look and see.

This elephant is big—
bigger than a man.
But...

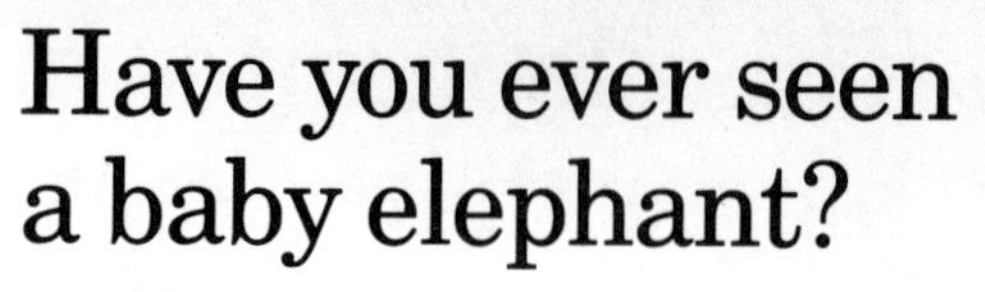

Have you ever seen
a baby elephant?

This man is big—
bigger than a baby elephant.

What's small?
Look and see.
This dog is small—

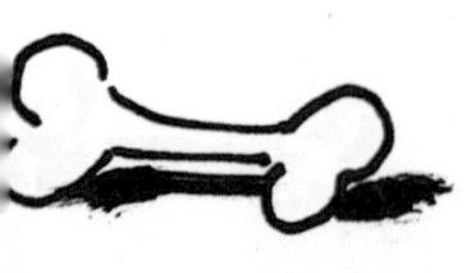

smaller than a lady.
But...

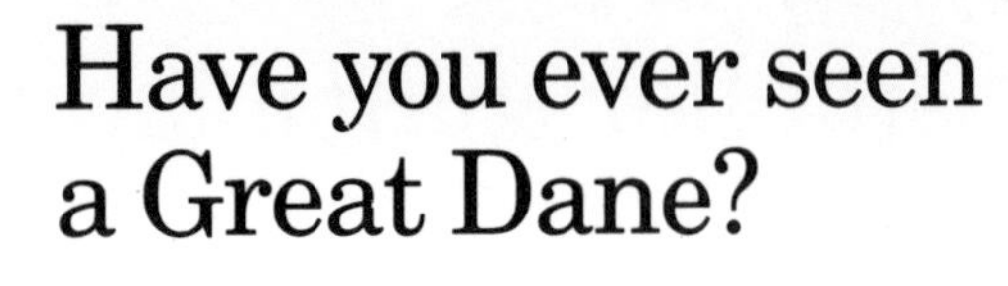

Have you ever seen
a Great Dane?

This man is small—
smaller than a Great Dane.

What's bigger
than an elephant?

Dinosaurs are bigger.

Whales are bigger
than elephants.

Airplanes are bigger
than whales and elephants.

Skyscrapers are bigger
than airplanes and
whales and elephants.

What's smaller
than a dog?

Rabbits are smaller
than dogs.

Mice are smaller
than rabbits and dogs.

Most bugs are smaller
than mice and
rabbits and dogs.

Many things are smaller
than the smallest bugs.

What's the smallest thing you can find?

What's the biggest thing you can find?

A star?

The moon?

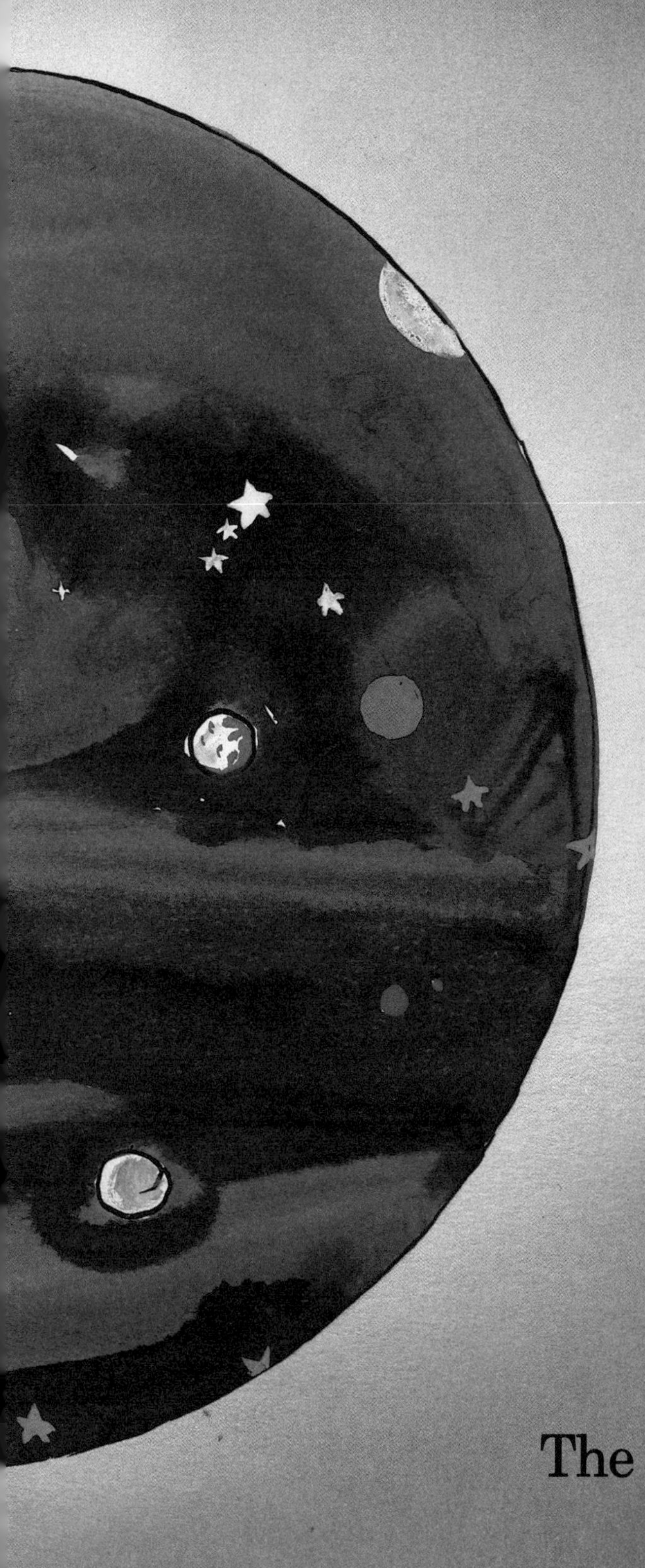

A planet?

The universe?

How small are you?